The Golem

Gaby Halberstam
Illustrated by Laura Clark

A & C Black • London

KNOWSLEY SCHOOL
LIBRARY SERVICE

White Wolves series consultant: Sue Ellis,
Centre for Literacy in Primary Education

This book can be used in the White Wolves Guided Reading
programme by more advanced readers in Year 2

First published 2012 by
A & C Black
Bloomsbury Publishing Plc
50 Bedford Square
London
WC1B 3DP

www.acblack.com

ISBN 978-1-4081-5577-6

A CIP catalogue for this book is available from the British Library.

Printed and bound in China by C & C Offset Printing Co.

1 3 5 7 9 10 8 6 4 2

Chapter One

Hundreds of years ago in the beautiful city of Prague, the Jewish people lived huddled together near the banks of the Vlatava River, in a place called the ghetto.

Outside, the crocuses were blooming and the air hummed with new life.

But inside the synagogue, where the Jews went to pray, the people were worried. And they all came to Rabbi Judah Loew.

"Rabbi," said a boy with wide eyes. "People are telling horrible lies about us. They say we're monsters. Why are they saying such awful things?"

Rabbi Judah had also heard these lies. Some people outside the ghetto believed them and could be very cruel.

"Rabbi," the old lady with the humped back whispered. "I have heard that they are going to attack us."

Rabbi Judah was very frightened. He wanted to find a way to protect his people.

Chapter Two

That night, he tossed and turned in his bed. He prayed that his people would be safe, but he had horrible dreams all night.

"Help! Please help us!" he cried out in his sleep.

A sudden bright light filled his room, startling Rabbi Judah wide awake. He watched as the light shrank until it formed one word that glowed briefly against the darkness:

Golem!

Rabbi Judah shook with fear and wonder. A golem was a giant, made from mud and clay. But how could he find a golem?

Could he create one?

Rabbi Judah thought about the danger to his people, and how they'd begged him for help.

And he was sure that he had received an answer to his prayers.

Chapter Three

He rose from his bed, and gathering his cloak around him, he called for his son-in-law, Isaac, and his wisest student, Jacob, to help him.

They bathed, and dressed themselves in white clothes.

Then, with the night still dark enough to hide them, they slipped through the silent streets of the ghetto and made their way to the river.

Under the glittering stars, using their bàre hands, the three men began to dig.

Together they sculpted the cold, thick clay into the shape of a giant man. For a moment, Rabbi Judah, Isaac and Jacob gazed at the golem lying in front of them on the river bank.

Then Isaac walked seven times around the body, chanting special words, and the clay burned bright red.

Jacob walked seven times around the golem, murmuring the special words. This time water flowed into and over the body. The men watched open-mouthed as the golem's fingers and toes grew nails.

Finally, Rabbi Judah walked around the golem. At its head, he stopped. He bowed to the east, to the west, to the south and to the north.

Chanting, Rabbi Judah leant over the peaceful body of the golem and, using his finger, he wrote the word *emet* – the Hebrew word for 'truth' – on the golem's forehead.

Just as he was completing the final letter, an icy wind rose from the river. With a high-pitched howl, it hurled itself at the three men, clawing their faces, and spattering their white clothes with dark red mud.

The clay beneath their feet bubbled and churned. Jacob and Isaac hid behind Rabbi Judah. Lightning forked the sky, and the body of the golem shuddered. Thunder rumbled from deep inside his chest, and...

...the golem opened his eyes.

Chapter Four

The wind turned into a sigh, the clay under their feet became smooth, and the sky softened to the gentle shades of dawn. A distant rooster crowed.

Rabbi Judah reached for the golem's hand.
Together, the three men helped him to his
feet, and led him to the ghetto.

The golem was tall, broad and strong. He never spoke, but he had powerful arms and legs and bright, burning eyes.

By day and by night, he strode around the ghetto. His head and shoulders could be seen above the walls from far away.

Chapter Five

At first, the people outside the ghetto were
scared of the golem and left the Jews alone.

But after a while, the outsiders felt braver.

One Sabbath, a group of them stormed
into the ghetto shouting and waving sticks.
The golem grabbed their clubs as if they were
matches and flung them over his shoulder.
The outsiders ran away.

The next Sabbath, a big gang of outsiders came in with blazing torches. But with one huge breath, the golem blew out all the flames.

The mob ran away again. But this time the angry golem stomped out of the ghetto and chased after them. The loud thud of his steps echoed through the streets of Prague.

Standing in the synagogue, Rabbi Judah was horrified. He realised now that when he had made the golem, he had made a terrible mistake.

How could he stop the monster he had created?

He picked up his prayer book. It fell open at Psalm 92, a song of praise.

He and his people had all begun to sing when the golem's footsteps were heard once again. Louder and louder, faster and faster. People outside were calling for help.

Chapter Six

Rabbi Judah ran out of the synagogue.

The golem burst through the walls of the ghetto, waving an uprooted tree like a club.

"Golem!" Rabbi Judah shouted, stepping into his path and waving his hands.

The golem stopped. Breathing heavily, he leant over the rabbi.

Rabbi Judah reached up. With his fingers he erased one letter of the word on the golem's forehead, changing *emet* to *met*, the Hebrew word for 'death'.

The golem's eyes flashed brightly for a second, then the light in them faded. His shoulders sagged and his legs buckled. Then the breath left his body, and he slumped down and turned into a heap of cold, thick clay.

Rabbi Judah called for Jacob and Isaac.
Together they carried the clay up to the attic
of the synagogue and laid it on the floor.
Rabbi Judah locked and bolted the door.
He took the key, and flung it into the dark
water of the river. Then he returned to the
synagogue where his people were still waiting.

Together they sang Psalm 92 once again. And to this day, in memory of the interruption to that Sabbath service hundreds of years ago, Rabbi Judah's synagogue is the only place in the world where the Psalm is sung twice.

And as for the clay body of the golem, it is said that it lies still locked away in the attic – waiting to be brought to life once again.